BOOK
1

Little
OLYMPiANS

ZEUS, GOD OF THUNDER

little bee books

New York, NY
Interior designed by Natalie Padberg Bartoo
Manufactured in China RRD 0121
First Edition
10 9 8 7 6 5 4 3 2 1
Library of Congress Cataloging-in-Publication Data
Names: Newton, A.I., author. | Sarkar, Anjan, illustrator.
Title: Zeus, god of thunder / by A.I. Newton; illustrated by Anjan Sarkar.
Description: First edition. | New York, NY: Little Bee Books, [2021]
Series: Little Olympians; #1 | Audience: Ages 6-8 | Audience: Grades 2-3
Summary: Zeus causes a ruckus while living with his parents, Kronos and
Rhea, when every time he sneezes or gets mad his lightning shoots out, so
they send him to Eureka, a camp where little gods learn to use their super-
natural abilities, and with the help of other gods like the wise Athena and the
wisecracking Hermes, little Zeus learns to control his own powers and
succeed. Identifiers: LCCN 2020048662 | Subjects: CYAC: Zeus (Greek
deity)—Fiction. | Gods, Greek—Fiction. | Mythology, Greek—Fiction. |
Ability—Fiction. Classification: LCC PZ7.1.L4428 Ze 2021 | DDC [E]—dc23
LC record available at https://lccn.loc.gov/2020048662
ISBN 978-1-4998-1149-0 (pb)
First Edition 10 9 8 7 6 5 4 3 2 1
ISBN 978-1-4998-1148-3 (hc)
First Edition 10 9 8 7 6 5 4 3 2 1
ISBN 978-1-4998-1235-0 (ebook)
littlebeebooks.com
For information about special discounts on bulk purchases,
please contact Little Bee Books at sales@littlebeebooks.com.

Little Olympians

ZEUS, GOD OF THUNDER

BY A.I. NEWTON   ILLUSTRATED BY ANJAN SARKAR

BOOK 1

little bee books

TABLE OF CONTENTS

THE GODS OF OLYMPUS

Once, all-powerful gods ruled from their home atop the cloud-covered heights of Mount Olympus: Zeus, God of Thunder; Athena, Goddess of Wisdom; Apollo, God of Music and Poetry; Ares, God of Combat; Aphrodite, Goddess of Beauty and Nature; Poseidon, God of the Seas, and others possessed incredible powers, and controlled the fate of humans on Earth . . .

. . . but these powerful beings were not always the mighty gods of Olympus. Once, long ago, they were just a bunch of kids. . . .

CHAPTER 1
THUNDER AND LIGHTNING

"AAAAA-CHOOOOO!!"

A thunderous sneeze shattered the morning quiet in a palace on Mount Olympus. Lightning bolts bounced off the palace's gleaming, white marble walls. One bolt struck a portrait of Rhea the Titan, the mother of the boy who had sneezed. The gold-framed painting crashed to the floor.

"Zeus!" bellowed Kronos the Titan, the boy's father, and the ruler of Mount Olympus. "You must learn to control your powers. Last week, you destroyed all our jugs, bowls, and other pottery."

"But, Dad—"

"Before that, you almost blew up my golden carriage, you burned down your mother's favorite fig tree, and you blasted a hole in the front door of the palace!" Kronos shouted.

"But, Dad, I just had to sneeze and—"

Zeus stopped short when he saw his mother enter the room.

Rhea spotted her smashed-up portrait on the floor and noticed the black scorch marks on the walls.

"Zeus, my son, you have great power," she said.

"That's right," Zeus quickly replied. "I can create lightning and thunder. Watch!"

The boy clapped his hands and a great rumbling shook the palace, followed by a deafening crack of thunder. A nearby shelf shook, and an ancient statue tumbled toward the floor.

CLAP!

Kronos dropped to his knees and caught the statue just before it hit the hard marble. He returned the statue to its shelf.

"Yes," said Kronos, turning back to Zeus. "You can *create* lightning and thunder, but you cannot *control* it. There is a huge difference, one that makes you a serious danger to yourself and to everyone around you."

"Not to mention to everything in this palace," Rhea said, smiling.

"I'm trying," Zeus whined. "I really am!"

Although Zeus was quite old in human years—over a hundred, in fact—in god years, he looked and acted like an eight-year-old boy.

"Trying is simply not enough!" Kronos thundered.

"Your father is right," Rhea added. "Powers like yours are not easy to control. In time, you may grow up to become the most powerful god of all. But for now—"

"You just don't trust me!" Zeus cried, then he stamped his foot, pulled open the heavy wooden front door, and stormed out of the palace.

Outside, Zeus sat on the massive front steps. He looked up at the palace's glistening marble columns rising high into the swirling clouds. He then stared at the barren rocky cliffs that surrounded him.

Why do they make me feel like I can't do anything right? he thought. *I know I messed up, but it's just not—*

"Zeus!" boomed Kronos from inside the palace. "Please come in here."

Zeus jumped. His dad had such a loud, deep voice that it sometimes felt like he was yelling at Zeus, even when Zeus knew he really wasn't. Zeus laughed to himself and headed back inside.

"Your mother and I have come to a decision," Kronos said firmly once Zeus had returned. "The time has come for you to leave home and go to Eureka!"

CHAPTER 2

JOURNEY TO EUREKA

"It's not fair!" Zeus shouted. "I'm a hundred and twelve years old! And you treat me like I'm a baby!"

"Zeus, all young gods go to Eureka to train and learn how to control their powers," Rhea explained. "You're just going a little earlier than we had planned. At Eureka, you'll be taught by mentors, including the older gods who have chosen to remain there to help train younger gods."

"Your older brother Poseidon is one of them," Kronos added. "He'll help you learn to control your powers."

"Yes," added Rhea, "and your brother Hades is also there training to hone his abilities."

"I guess so," Zeus said, realizing that he had no choice. Kronos and Rhea hugged him, then Zeus went off to pack.

A short while later, Zeus loaded a tapestry bag filled with clothes and books into a golden carriage. The carriage was hitched up to a team of six flying horses, which were led by Pegasus.

"Learn well, my son," said Rhea, kissing Zeus goodbye on his forehead.

"Listen to your brother Poseidon," added Kronos. "He will help you at Eureka."

Zeus climbed into the carriage, grabbed the reins, and shouted, "Skyward, Pegasus!"

The six horses flapped their feathered wings, lifting themselves, the carriage, and Zeus into the sky.

After a journey of several hours, a mountaintop came into view, poking up through the clouds.

"There it is!" Zeus shouted, starting to get excited about his new adventure. "All right, Pegasus, lead me to Eureka."

The flying horses guided the carriage to the mountaintop, landing in a clearing near a forest.

Zeus climbed out of the carriage and grabbed his bag. He looked around, but saw no one.

"Where is Poseidon?" he wondered aloud. "Father told me he would be here to greet me."

Suddenly, Zeus heard the sound of galloping hooves coming from the forest. The pounding grew louder, then a strange-looking creature—half man, half horse—burst out from the trees and charged right at him!

CHAPTER 3

THE MENTOR

Startled, Zeus instinctively raised his hands. Lightning bolts shot from his fingertips, slamming into the side of a nearby cliff. Chunks of rock broke off, crashing to the ground just in front of the charging half man, half horse. The creature skidded to a stop right in front of Zeus.

"Well, that's not the greeting I usually get," said the being, brushing the dirt from his shoulders. "I'm guessing that you must be Zeus."

Zeus nodded proudly.

"Allow me to introduce myself," said the half man, half horse. "I am Centaur the Mentor."

Centaur paused and smiled at Zeus, who looked even more baffled than he already was.

"Hmm . . . that line usually gets a laugh from young gods," said Centaur.

"I'm confused," Zeus said. "I thought my brother was supposed to meet me here."

"You will see Poseidon soon enough," said Centaur. "I am here to welcome you to Eureka. I have been training young gods for many years, including your brother. He has become one of my best assistants. And honestly, Poseidon is really quite excited that you are here."

"He is?" Zeus asked, looking shocked. "He never paid much attention to me at home."

"Hmm . . . older brothers," said Centaur. "I have one myself. Don't get me started. But now if you please, follow me."

Centaur trotted back into the forest. As Zeus hurried to follow him, he heard the sound of the flying horses flapping their wings and taking off into the sky.

I guess they're heading back to Mount Olympus, Zeus thought. *Looks like I'm going to be here for a while.*

As he walked along a dirt path, Zeus heard pounding footsteps behind him. He turned and saw two young boys run by.

"Out of the way, newbie!" shouted one of the boys as Zeus jumped from the path into some bushes. Centaur rolled his eyes and calmly stepped off the path.

"Unless you think you can run faster than us!" the other boy shouted as he passed Zeus.

Before Zeus could figure out what was going on, another boy came running up the path, coming from the same direction as the first two.

"Showing off for a newbie again?" shouted the third boy. "Well, I can run faster than the both of you!" Picking up speed, he rushed by Zeus and Centaur, then flew right past the first two boys. Within seconds, the three runners had vanished from sight.

"Who are those kids?" Zeus asked.

"Ah," said Centaur. "The first two are Apollo and Ares. They are inseparable. They are also the two best athletes in all of Eureka."

"That last kid was *really* fast!" Zeus said, impressed and a little intimidated.

"That is Hermes," said Centaur, "and, yes, he is the swiftest of all the gods. I have a feeling that you two might get along well."

Zeus and Centaur continued onward, soon emerging from the forest and stepping out onto a gleaming white sand beach. The mighty ocean roared as waves crashed against the shore.

Apollo, Ares, and Hermes came running along the beach right up to Zeus. But before they could say a word, a powerful voice shouted over the sounds of the ocean.

"ZEUS!!!" the voice boomed.

Zeus turned and looked out at the ocean. His eyes opened wide at what he saw.

THE BIG BROTHER

CHAPTER 4

A familiar-looking god riding on the back of a dolphin burst from the ocean, surfing along on top of an enormous wave. Looking on from the shore, Zeus saw that from the waist up, the god looked no different from him. But below his belly, this god had a fish-like tail covered in scales. In his right hand, he held a trident, raising it above his head as he roared, "Zeus! You finally made it!"

"Poseidon!" Zeus shouted, realizing suddenly that this strange-looking being was his big brother!

He turned to Centaur.

"I always knew that Poseidon had a strong connection to the sea," Zeus said. "He was always a great swimmer, and he seemed to somehow be able to communicate with sea creatures. But he always had legs. Now, he looks like he's part fish!"

Poseidon rode the wave all the way to shore. He leapt from the dolphin, who turned and dove back into the ocean. While in midair, Poseidon's mer-tail transformed into legs and his trident changed into a gnarled, old walking stick.

"Welcome, little brother!" Poseidon boomed, grasping Zeus by his shoulders. "You have made it to Eureka, and I will see to it that you become the best god you can be. Like me!"

Zeus stared down at his older brother's feet.

"But . . . you had a tail," he said, pointing. "Like a-a-a well, like a fish!"

"Correct, little brother," said Poseidon. "Thanks to my training here at Eureka, my true powers have emerged. In water, my tail appears, making me a powerful swimmer; while back on land, I have legs like I've always had. This requires control and focus. Both of which you will learn now that you are here."

Apollo, Ares, and Hermes walked over to Zeus.

"I'm Hermes," said one, extending his hand. "Welcome to Eureka!"

Zeus shook Hermes's hand.

"I'm Ares," said the other. "And if you want to learn about strength . . ."

". . . or fighting," Apollo added.

". . . or winning at any athletic competition," said Ares.

"Watch us," said Apollo. "And try your best to keep up."

"Just don't try to keep up with their bragging," Hermes said, putting his arm around Zeus. "'Cause that's what they're *really* good at!"

Apollo and Ares do seem pretty full of themselves, Zeus thought.

Poseidon laughed loudly. Apollo and Ares frowned and folded their arms across their chests.

"Enough!" Centaur said loudly. "The time for training has come. Everyone—to the Power Circle!"

Centaur turned and galloped back into the forest.

"The Power Circle?" Zeus asked.

"Follow me," said Poseidon. "And pay close attention. Your silly days as a reckless young god are over. Mother and Father have told me about all the destruction you've been causing."

Poseidon turned and walked into the forest.

Does everyone here know all the trouble I've had controlling my powers? Zeus wondered. He hurried after Poseidon, wondering what exactly he was getting into.

CHAPTER 5

THE POWER CIRCLE

"So, what did Mom and Dad tell you about me?" Zeus asked as he and Poseidon walked through the forest.

"That you have started to show signs of having great power," his brother said. "But that you have not shown any ability to control it."

"I've been trying, but it's hard! Were you able to control your powers when you were my age?" Zeus asked.

Poseidon was 168 in god years, but he looked like a twelve-year-old boy.

"Not very well," Poseidon admitted. "But then again, my powers didn't cause quite as much damage as yours! The truth is, I did not truly learn to control my powers until I came here to Eureka and took part in training. Speaking of which . . ."

The two brothers stepped into a large, circular clearing next to a big lake. Zeus saw young gods practicing, supervised by older ones. Apollo, Ares, and Hermes, followed by Centaur, entered the clearing a moment later.

Across the circle, a young god named Athena worked with a group of recent arrivals. She guided them through a series of movements and breathing exercises.

"These exercises will help with your mental focus," said Athena. "And that is the key to controlling your power, no matter what it may be."

The students all raised their arms and took a deep breath.

"Good," said Athena. "Now, lower your arms slowly and exhale."

As the group followed her directions, a blast of fierce wind suddenly blew across the Power Circle. It slammed against a tree, snapping off a branch, which tumbled toward Zeus.

"Look out!" shouted Hermes.

Zeus looked up, frozen in place.

An arrow streaked through the air and pierced the branch, sticking it firmly into the tree trunk. The branch dangled right above Zeus's head.

He spun around to see who had saved him and saw one of Athena's students holding a bow. She had a quiver of arrows strapped across her back.

"Wow!" said Zeus. "That was incredible. Who is she?"

"That is Artemis," explained Poseidon. "She is Apollo's twin sister. She is just as talented and smart as he is. The difference is, she lets her *skill* do the talking."

43

"Nicely done, Artemis," said Athena. "Your quick action saved our newest arrival from quite a headache."

"I felt focused," Artemis said. "As if I knew exactly when to release the arrow."

Athena turned to another of her young students, Boreas, God of the North Wind. He just stared at the ground.

"Tell me what you felt just before you brought forth that wind," Athena said.

"I was kind of scared," Boreas explained. "I wanted to do well, but I was nervous that I would fail. I guess I tried too hard."

Zeus leaned in close to Poseidon. "That's how I feel sometimes when I can't control my lightning," he whispered.

"That's why you're here," Poseidon replied.

Athena put her hand on Boreas's shoulder.

"You must learn to trust your breathing and your movement," she said. Then she looked across the Power Circle. "You too, young Zeus."

"She heard me?" Zeus asked Poseidon, a bit embarrassed. "She's got good hearing."

"Yes, I do," said Athena. "Another benefit of learning how to focus."

Centaur stepped to the center of the Power Circle. "It is time for all of you to meet our newest student," he said. "This is Zeus. He can create lightning and thunder."

"Pretty cool," said Hermes.

"No big deal," mumbled Apollo.

"Step forward, Zeus," said Centaur.

Zeus walked nervously to the center of the Power Circle.

"The time for you to start your training has arrived, young Zeus," said Centaur. "Let us begin."

"I am ready!" Zeus announced loudly. *At least I hope I am!*

CHAPTER 6

ZEUS'S TRAINING BEGINS

Zeus stood in the ruins of a round, marble pavilion. With him were Apollo, Artemis, Ares, and Hermes. Tall columns, some still standing and some broken into pieces, surrounded them on a circular floor. If there ever had been a roof on this structure, it was long gone.

"The Pavilion is another one of our training locations," Centaur explained. "Here, Poseidon will lead you through a series of exercises."

"Today, we will work on your physical abilities," Poseidon explained. "We begin with the column climb."

The five young gods each stood before a tall column.

"On my mark, begin your climb," said Poseidon. "Focus your mind to work together with your arms and legs. Begin!"

Zeus wrapped his arms around the column and pulled himself up. At the same time, he pressed his feet against the column and pushed.

This is hard! he thought. *And I don't get what this has to do with controlling my powers.*

"Hey, Zeus!" Apollo shouted from a column next to his. "How's the view from down there?"

"It's pretty good from way up here," added Ares.

Zeus saw that Apollo and Ares were much farther up their columns than he was.

"You're supposed to climb with your arms and legs, not your mouth," shouted Hermes from his column. But he too, was way above Zeus.

"Don't worry about my big-shot brother," shouted Artemis, who was just as high up on her column as Apollo. "This is not a race. Just focus on what *you* need to do."

I just hope Poseidon doesn't think this is a race, Zeus thought.

He took a deep breath and continued up the column. By the time he reached the top, the others were already on their way down. When Zeus returned to the ground, he rejoined the group.

"I thought we'd have to wait all day for you," said Apollo.

"It's not a race," Zeus said, glancing at Artemis, who smiled at him. He looked over at Poseidon, whose face showed no emotion.

"Let us continue," Poseidon said.

Poseidon led the group through a series of speed and strength exercises. In all of these, Zeus could not keep up with the others.

It's not a race. It's not a competition, Zeus kept reminding himself. *But still, I feel like I'm doing the worst.*

"Our exercises so far have been about individual effort," Poseidon announced. "I wanted to push each of you to use all your strength. This final exercise, however, combines strength, balance, and control—but most of all, teamwork. I call it the 'pyramid.'"

Poseidon stood Apollo and Ares next to each other, shoulder to shoulder.

"Hermes, you are next," Poseidon said. "Onto their shoulders!"

Taking a running start, Hermes leaped into the air. He landed with one foot on Apollo's shoulder, and one on Ares's. The three wobbled a bit, but managed to steady themselves.

"Zeus, it is your turn," Poseidon said. "You will jump and land on Hermes's shoulders. But not before you catch an arrow fired by Artemis. Go!"

Why did he have to give me the hardest part? Zeus thought, hesitating. *He has to push me harder, just because I'm his brother!*

"Zeus, go!" Poseidon shouted again.

Zeus raced across the pavilion. When he was five feet away from the three-man pyramid, he leaped into the air, tucking his legs up under him.

At that moment, Artemis fired an arrow toward Zeus. He reached up and snatched the speeding arrow out of the air.

Got it! he thought, pleased with the quickness of his own reflexes. *Now for the hard part.*

Zeus dropped his feet down, aiming for Hermes's shoulders. He landed, but he struggled to get his balance.

I'm going to fall! he thought.

Panic overwhelmed Zeus, causing him to release a lightning bolt that supercharged the arrow in his hand. The sizzling arrow flew back toward Artemis.

"Artemis, look out!" Zeus shouted as the whole pyramid toppled to the ground.

Artemis ducked, and the flaming arrow passed inches from her head.

"Nice going, newbie," said Apollo, rolling off the others. "Maybe you should have stayed home with Mommy and Daddy."

Zeus looked out from the bottom of the pile. He saw Poseidon shaking his head and turning away.

I'm never going to get this. In fact, I'm never going to use my powers again, he thought.

CHAPTER 7

FRIENDS AND FOES

Later that day, Zeus stretched out on his bed. The young gods being trained in Eureka stayed in the ruins of a former temple. The teachers and mentors there nicknamed it "the bunkhouse."

Zeus stared up at the ceiling. *Maybe I'm just not meant to be the god my parents, Poseidon, and everyone else wants me to be.*

Zeus's thoughts were interrupted by a loud knock on the door.

*Probably Poseidon coming to lecture
me.*

"Go away!" he shouted.

"Is that any way to treat your friends?"
said a familiar voice from the other side
of the door.

"Hermes?" asked Zeus, getting up and
opening the door.

Hermes and Athena smiled at Zeus.

"We wanted to make sure that you're
okay," said Athena.

"Yeah," added Hermes. "We figured you were pretty down on yourself, so we came to lift you up—um, but not literally—I'm still a bit sore," he joked, rubbing his shoulder.

"Sorry about that," said Zeus. "I tried, but I just can't. . . . I don't think I should use my powers again. It's not safe."

"Don't say that. It's all part of the learning process," said Athena. "You should have seen Hermes when he first got here. Mister Fastest God There Is was tripping over his own feet!"

"Hey!" Hermes said, pretending to be upset. "You don't have to give away all my secrets!"

"Slow down," Athena said to Zeus. "You can't rush learning. You need to move slowly, focus your mind, then channel your power through that focus. In time, this method of control will become just like second nature."

Zeus nodded.

"You can imagine how hard that advice was to follow for a speedster like me! So, I know you'll get the hang of it eventually," said Hermes.

"Hey, I have an idea," Athena said.

She grabbed a candle that was burning on a nearby table.

"Before you try to control lightning, how about trying to control a simple form of fire?" she said. "Focus your mind on the candle's flame, then raise your hands slowly. See if you can make the flame move."

Zeus closed his eyes and took a deep breath. As he exhaled, he lifted his hands and opened his eyes.

"Focus on the flame," repeated Athena. Zeus thought hard about the flame, picturing it in his mind. At first, nothing happened. But after a few tries, the candle bent slightly to the right.

"Good! Try it again, only this time, take several breaths and spend more time thinking about the flame."

Zeus nodded. He took a few deep breaths and again focused his mind on the candle—both its flame and its heat. This time the flame grew, extending three feet up into the air. Zeus started to panic.

"Relax, Zeus," said Athena. "Stay calm. Now bring the flame back down to its normal size."

Zeus lowered his hands and the flame returned to normal.

"Great!" said Athena. "That's a terrific first step."

"I did it!" Zeus smiled. He started to feel a little better.

Another knock came at the door.

"Come in," said Zeus.

In walked Artemis, leaving the door open behind her.

"Hey, nice catch of that arrow," said Artemis. "You've got decent reflexes."

"I'm sorry about the flaming arrow thing afterward," said Zeus.

"Forget it," said Artemis. "I never mind a little extra excitement."

"Athena said that all I need is to slow down," Zeus explained.

"I don't know how anyone could be any slower," said a voice from the hallway.

Zeus looked over and saw Apollo and Ares appear in his doorway.

"How come we weren't invited to this party?" Ares asked, pretending to be insulted.

"Oh, I don't know," said Hermes. "Maybe it's because you haven't said a single nice thing to Zeus since he got here?"

Zeus laughed. "Well, there's a first time for everything," he said, happy that once again, Hermes had his back.

"At least you won't have to worry about messing up tomorrow," said Apollo. "We were just watching Poseidon do a demonstration with the advanced class. And rumor has it that he's bringing a very special guest—a Cyclops!"

Zeus's eyes opened wide. He'd heard about the legendary one-eyed giants, but he had never actually seen one.

"Wow!" Zeus said.

"Enough talk," said Ares. "It's time for dinner."

"Last one to the dining room has to clean all the dishes!" said Hermes, dashing out of the room past Apollo and Ares.

The other young gods all ran after him.

CHAPTER 8

THE ADVANCED CLASS

The next morning, Zeus met up with Hermes, Athena, Apollo, Ares, and Artemis. The group headed to the Twisting Caves Training Area, site of the advanced class led by Poseidon.

"I'm excited to see Poseidon's students at work," added Athena.

At least he won't be disappointed in me again, since I'm only watching, thought Zeus.

"There's the entrance," said Artemis, pointing to a narrow opening in the face of a rocky cliff.

The young gods entered and wound their way through a series of caves connected by narrow passageways. The last passageway opened into a huge, high-ceilinged cave that came complete with an underground lake.

"Wow!" said Zeus as he and his friends gathered at the edge of the lake. "This place is amazing."

Across the lake on the opposite shore, Poseidon gathered with his students—Dionysus, God of Growing Things; Hestia, God of Family and Hearth; and Hades, God of the Underworld, with his three-headed puppy, Cerberus.

"Welcome, students and observers," Poseidon began. "Today, you will learn how to think on your feet and to make quick decisions. There are many evil creatures in the realms of Mount Olympus and here at Eureka." Poseidon continued, "Among them is the Cyclops."

Zeus felt a surge of excitement at the mention of the monster's name.

"I know for a fact that a Cyclops lives in these caves," Poseidon said, pausing to let this sink in. "In fact, he lives in *that* tunnel."

Poseidon pointed to an arched tunnel opening which was closed off by a heavy iron gate.

"Today, we will open the gate and engage the monster in direct combat. The goal is to return the Cyclops to its tunnel and re-close the gate."

Zeus felt as if he could almost touch the tension rippling through the cave.

"Novices, take your places!" Poseidon commanded.

Dionysus, Hestia, and Hades and Cerberus positioned themselves around the cave.

Poseidon grabbed the tunnel gate and slowly slid it open. The sound of iron scraping on stone filled the cave.

A mighty roar echoed from deep inside the tunnel. The students all braced themselves.

What if they can't stop him? Zeus worried, feeling afraid for the first time since he had arrived at Eureka.

Poseidon and the rest of the novices braced for battle. A few seconds later, the Cyclops appeared at the entrance to the tunnel. The monster stood twelve feet tall, with a muscular body and one large round eye in the middle of his forehead.

"Behold the Cyclops!" Poseidon shouted.

The Cyclops roared, and then he charged right at Poseidon!

ENTER THE CYCLOPS

CHAPTER 9

The Cyclops lumbered toward Poseidon.

"He is powerful, but he is also slow and clumsy!" Poseidon shouted to his students. "We can use that to our advantage."

Poseidon easily sidestepped the monster's charge. From her perch on a high ledge, Hestia tossed a large stone at the Cyclops. It struck him on the arm, sending him stumbling to the side—right toward Cerberus.

The three-headed puppy leapt onto the Cyclops's back. He growled, revealing three sets of sharp teeth. But before he could attack, the Cyclops reached back, grabbed Cerberus, and tossed him aside.

Hades caught his beloved pet before he hit the ground.

With anger flashing in his eyes, Hades charged at the monster.

"You mess with Cerberus, you mess with me, big guy!" Hades shouted.

The Cyclops easily snatched him up and squeezed him in a powerful fist.

"Dionysus!" Poseidon shouted, fearing for his brother. "There!"

Poseidon pointed at a small patch of moss growing on a damp rock. Dionysus, who had a strong connection to plants and trees, closed his eyes and focused directly on the moss.

The green patch lifted off the rock, flew through the air, and landed on the Cyclops's eye, temporarily blinding him.

The Cyclops roared and dropped Hades, who scrambled to safety. Then the Cyclops reached up and peeled the moss off his eye.

Poseidon snuck up behind the monster and hooked his walking stick around one of the Cyclops's ankles. Yanking hard on the stick, he caused the Cyclops to trip and fall flat on his face, right at the shoreline of the underground lake.

Poseidon focused his powers on the lake. A creature, covered in scales, tentacles, and suction cups, rose from the water. Following Poseidon's command, the creature grabbed the Cyclops's arms and legs with its long tentacles and dragged him into the lake. They both vanished under the surface of the water.

Zeus stared at the lake's surface. *Is it over? Did that creature beat the Cyclops?*

Zeus got his answer when, a few seconds later, the lake creature came flying out of the water. Poseidon caught the creature and gently tossed it back into the lake.

The Cyclops started to climb from the lake, sloshing his way toward the shore.

Leaping into the air, Poseidon tackled the Cyclops, dragging him back underwater.

"Where are they?" Zeus asked, as the cave became still.

Tense seconds later, the Cyclops and Poseidon broke the water's surface, grappling in a powerful struggle.

"Our turn!" shouted Hades, diving into the water.

Hestia and Dionysus joined him, but the three were quickly tossed back onto the shore.

"Poseidon!" Zeus cried.

The Cyclops emerged, holding Poseidon above his head. Then he tossed the god from the lake.

Poseidon landed hard on the rocky shore just as his mer-tail morphed back into legs. He tried to pull himself to his feet, but his right leg gave out and he crumbled to the rocks. The Cyclops climbed out of the lake and moved menacingly toward the seemingly helpless god.

Dionysus, Hestia, and Hades and Cerberus ran to help Poseidon. Seeing this, the Cyclops lifted an enormous boulder and tossed it at the young gods. The boulder hit the ground and rolled toward them like an enormous bowling ball.

The young gods dove into a cave for cover, but when the boulder stopped, it blocked the entrance to the cave.

"They're trapped!" Zeus shouted. He looked on in horror at the prospect of his big brother being defeated—or worse—by the monster. The other advanced students couldn't help. As Zeus's fear mounted, small jolts of lightning flashed from his fingers, sizzling on the damp rocks below his hands.

I feel so helpless!

CHAPTER 10

FRIENDLY COMPETITORS

Zeus turned to Athena and Hermes.

"The advanced students are trapped!" he said. "We're the only ones who can help Poseidon now. But I'm scared. What if I accidentally hurt my brother instead?"

"I'm on it," said Hermes. "When the time comes, you'll know what to do." Then he sped off, running at top speed right at the Cyclops.

Athena took Zeus's hands.

"Remember what I taught you," she whispered. "Remember the candle and the flame. Slow down. Breathe. Focus. Your power is an extension of who you are. Use that to help your brother."

Zeus looked across the lake and saw Hermes running back and forth in front of the Cyclops.

"Hey, big guy, bet you can't catch me!" Hermes shouted.

The Cyclops started chasing Hermes, who led the monster away from the injured Poseidon.

Zeus closed his eyes and extended his hands. *Focus,* he told himself. *Focus. My power works through me.*

Zeus opened his eyes and looked up at the rocky cave roof just ahead of where Hermes was leading the Cyclops. He imagined lightning and the power of its electricity. Then he felt a familiar tingling in his fingertips.

I know what Hermes wants me to do! But this has to be timed just right.

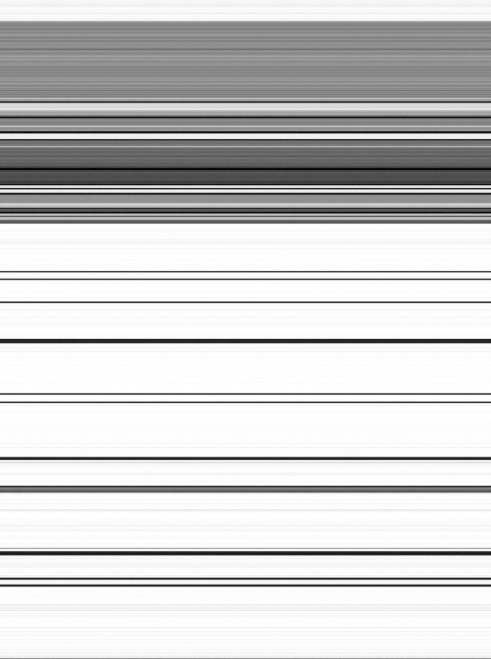

Having fin -

Dionysus, Hes t

Poseidon and H

"I'm all right,

my head. Lef t

minutes. But n

Quickly!"

Dionysus, He

the unconscio

him back to the

Then, working

the iron gate cl

He took a deep breath, then unleashed a powerful, but tightly controlled, lightning bolt at the roof. The bolt streaked above the lake and struck the roof a few feet ahead of the Cyclops. Large chunks of rock broke off and came crashing down, right on Cyclops's head. The giant monster fell to the ground, unconscious.

Having finally freed themselves, Dionysus, Hestia, and Hades all rushed to Poseidon and helped him to his feet.

"I'm all right," he said. "Just a bump on my head. Left me dizzy for a couple of minutes. But now I need everyone's help. Quickly!"

Dionysus, Hestia, and Hades all grabbed the unconscious Cyclops and dragged him back to the tunnel he had come from. Then, working as a team, they slammed the iron gate closed.

Still a bit winded and sore from his struggle, Poseidon addressed his students.

"Today's class is over. Good work, all."

Then he pulled Zeus aside.

"Nice shot, little brother."

Zeus felt strong for the first time since arriving at Eureka.

That evening at dinner in the dining hall of the bunkhouse, Zeus sat with Hermes and Athena.

"Well, guess who turned out to be a hero?" said Athena.

"Oh, I know, I know," said Hermes. "Mister I'll Never Use My Powers Again."

Zeus laughed.

"Thank you, guys," he said.

"One lucky shot," said Apollo from the next table, where he sat with Ares and Artemis.

"Well, that's one more than *you* had today!" said Hermes.

Zeus and his friends laughed. At the next table, even Apollo and Ares laughed. Zeus was happy to have made friends so quickly, and he was already looking forward to using his powers again for tomorrow's lessons.

Look for more books by these creators...

...and read on for a sneak peek at the second book in the Little Olympians series

CHAPTER 1

THE EUREKA OLYMPICS

Zeus, Athena, Aphrodite, Apollo, Artemis, Ares, and Hermes were young gods sent to Eureka by their parents to learn how to control their developing powers. One day, they all gathered around a long table in the dining room of the bunkhouse, their home away from home.

"That dinner was delicious!" said Zeus. Since arriving at Eureka for training several months earlier, Zeus's confidence in using his power of controlling thunder and lightning had grown.

"Yeah, but what's for dessert?" asked Hermes, the fastest of all the young gods at Eureka. "A meal is just not complete without dessert."

"It's a good thing you run as fast as you do," said Artemis, whose skill as an archer was improving every day. "With that sweet tooth of yours, you need a way to burn it all off."

"Well, we happen to have a very special dessert," said Athena. "Hestia, Goddess of Family and Hearth, baked us a fig and honey pie. You remember her. She was in the advanced group of gods that helped us battle the Cyclops."

"Ooh," said Hermes. "I've had her pies before. She is an excellent baker. Bring it on!"

Athena placed a still-steaming fig and honey pie in the center of the table. But before anyone could get a piece, the door to the bunkhouse flew open. In walked Centaur, a half man, half horse, who served as a mentor to the young gods at Eureka.

"Everyone is needed outside immediately for an important announcement," he said.

"Race you!" shouted Ares, bolting from the table.

Everyone else followed, trying to push past one another to be the first one out the door.

On the large stone patio in front of the bunkhouse, Centaur and Poseidon were waiting. Poseidon was Zeus's older brother and also a teacher at Eureka.

"I see you all remain quite competitive with each other, even in something as simple as leaving a building," said Centaur, once everyone had finally gathered. "But this is good, and Poseidon will tell you why."

Poseidon stepped forward to speak.

"Tomorrow morning, we begin a series of highly competitive games which we like to call the Eureka Olympics—a long-standing tradition we have here," Poseidon began. "These contests are designed to help you learn how to think quickly as you face unexpected situations. You will need to use your powers thoughtfully and swiftly to succeed. Until tomorrow morning, then."

The young gods returned to the bunkhouse dining room excited about the games.

"Well, you know if any of the games call for great speed, I'll be the winner," Hermes boasted through a mouthful of pie.

"As long as it isn't a contest of strength," Apollo chimed in.

"That's right," said Ares. "Because I'm going to win *that* contest!"

"No way!" Apollo said.

"I've gotten much better at aiming my lightning bolts," said Zeus. "So I hope one of the challenges involves hitting a target."

"If it does, I'll be right there with you," said Artemis, pulling an arrow from the quiver on her back, loading up her bow, and firing. The arrow streaked across the room, went right through the handle of a metal cup resting on a nearby table, and pinned the cup to the far wall.

"Well, if nature is involved in one of the games, that game will be mine!" said Aphrodite. She pointed a finger at a vining plant. The plant grew two feet taller in a matter of seconds.

Zeus noticed Athena sitting alone quietly as the others all boasted about their abilities.

"What about you, Athena?" Zeus asked. "What kind of game will you win?"

Before Athena could reply, Apollo jumped in: "I guess if there's a petteia match, she's got it made, being the Goddess of Wisdom and all." Apollo made air quotes with his fingers when he said the word "wisdom."

"My parents like to play petteia," said Zeus. "It's a really hard board game with lots of strategy involved. I couldn't even figure out how to make the first move."

Athena smiled, then got up and walked outside without saying a word.

"I hope she's okay," said Zeus, watching his friend leave.